OUT ON A LIMB

Words by
JORDAN MORRIS

Pictures by
CHARLIE MYLIE

Abrams Books for Young Readers
New York

Lulu surveyed her sympathy trove and smiled.

Two new games, three good books, six cards, a dozen daisies,

a slew of balloons, and a matching yellow cast for Bonnie Bear.

So far, Lulu mused, *this broken leg isn't so bad.*

Over the next week, Lulu had to think
of new ways to do ordinary things.

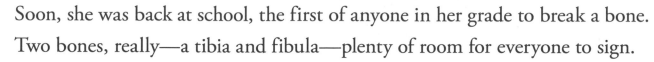

Soon, she was back at school, the first of anyone in her grade to break a bone.
Two bones, really—a tibia and fibula—plenty of room for everyone to sign.

Classmates wanted every detail: the accident, the ambulance, the X-ray, the flavor of hospital ice cream (strawberry).

Lulu only embellished a little.

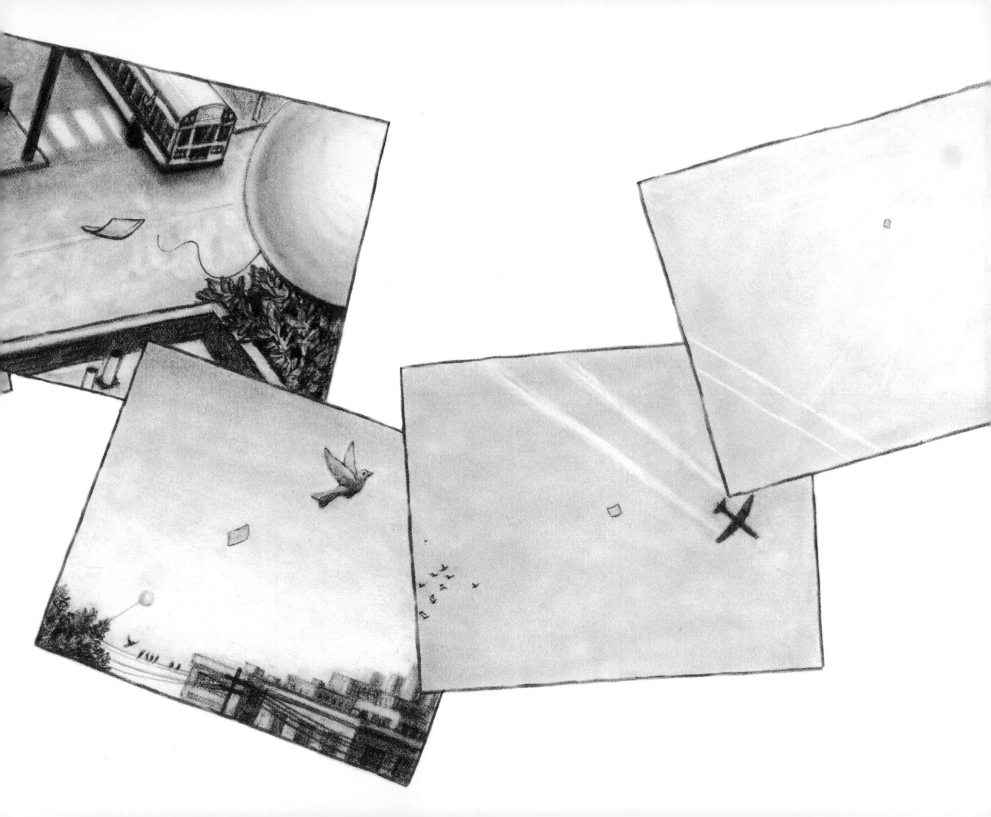

It wasn't long before all
of Lulu's special attention
evaporated.

By day, she grew bored,
grumpy, and restless.

By night, she tossed and turned. Her leg was sore—itchy and twitchy, trapped inside its yellow shell. In the dark, Lulu tapped, whacked, poked, and scratched.

After six weeks, Lulu and Bonnie visited the hospital again to have their casts removed.

Bonnie went first. Without her cast, she looked fluffy and new.

When it was Lulu's turn, she was afraid, even though it didn't hurt.

The nurse gently lifted Lulu's leg out of her cast and onto the table. Finally free.

Shouldn't she be happy to get rid of that itchy, old cast?

Looking down at her skinny leg, Lulu wasn't happy at all. She wondered if it could run, jump, and climb like before. She wondered if it would break again.

Over the next few days, everyone wanted Lulu to do something Lulu didn't want to do.

She wasn't ready to do things the ordinary way.

She wanted to be Lulu with a
yellow cast and she wanted her
leg to be safe inside.

That weekend, Grandpa came for a visit. He took Lulu to their favorite park, just like always.

"Let's climb to the top of the tower!"
said Grandpa, offering his hand.
Lulu shook her head. "No thanks, not today."

She scratched at the sand with a stick, watching other kids play soccer and tag.

Lulu wanted to climb the tower with Grandpa. She wanted to be fearless and fast, but she knew bad things could happen.

Walking home, Grandpa pulled
the wagon and whistled a tune.
"Did you get my letter yet?"
he asked, checking the mailbox.

Lulu shook her head. No letter.
"It must be lost forever," she said,
frowning.

"Maybe . . ." Grandpa smiled.
"But some things just need a little extra time."

The next day, Lulu swung in the sun, lifting her ear to a bird's happy little tune.

Peering up into the tree, she did not find the bird. Instead, she spied something unusual pinned into the crook of a branch.

After thinking it over for some time, curiosity made her brave and bravery made her climb.

For Mira
—J.M.

To the curious and brave, especially Misha
—C.M.

The illustrations were drawn in graphite on hot press paper, then colored and touched up digitally.

Library of Congress Cataloging-in-Publication Data
Names: Morris, Jordan, author. | Mylie, Charlie, illustrator.
Title: Out on a limb / by Jordan Morris ; illustrated by Charlie Mylie.
Description: New York, NY : Abrams Books for Young Readers, 2022. |
Audience: Ages 4 to 8 | Summary: Lulu does not mind having a broken leg while she is the center of attention,
but after the newness wears off, it takes a visit from Grandpa and a well-timed letter to set things right.
Identifiers: LCCN 2020044632 | ISBN 9781419753657 (hardcover) | ISBN
9781647002572 (ebook) Subjects: CYAC: Fractures—Fiction. | Grandfathers—Fiction. |
Letters—Fiction. | Self-confidence—Fiction.
Classification: LCC PZ7.1.M672757 Out 2022 | DDC [E]—dc23
LC record available at https://lccn.loc.gov/2020044632

Text © 2022 Jordan Morris
Illustrations © 2022 Charlie Mylie
Book design by Heather Kelly

Printed and bound in China
10 9 8 7 6 5 4 3 2 1

Abrams® is a registered trademark of Harry N. Abrams, Inc.

ABRAMS The Art of Books
195 Broadway, New York, NY 10007
abramsbooks.com